SADDLEBACK
PUBLISHING·INC.

Barclay Family Adventures

Danger at 20 Fathoms

6 ft.

BY

Ed Hanson

THE BARCLAY FAMILY ADVENTURES

BOOK 1: Amazon Adventure
BOOK 2: **Danger at 20 Fathoms**
BOOK 3: Desert Ordeal
BOOK 4: Forest Fire
BOOK 5: Hostages
BOOK 6: Lost at Sea
BOOK 7: Mountain Blizzard
BOOK 8: Tornado
BOOK 9: The Pass
BOOK 10: The Swamp

Development and Production: Laurel Associates, Inc.
Cover and Interior Art: Black Eagle Productions

SADDLEBACK PUBLISHING•INC.
Three Watson
Irvine, CA 92618-2767
E-Mail: info@sdlback.com
Website: www.sdlback.com

ISBN 1-56254-551-5

Printed in the United States of America
08 07 06 05 04 9 8 7 6 5 4 3 2 1

CONTENTS

MEET THE BARCLAYS

Paul Barclay

~ A fun-loving father of three who takes his kids on his travels whenever he can.

Ann Barclay

The devoted mother who manages the homefront during Paul's many absences as an on-site construction engineer. ~

Jim Barclay

~ The eldest child, Jim is a talented athlete with his eye on a football scholarship at a major college.

Aaron Barclay

Three years younger than Jim, he's inquisitive, daring, and an absolute whiz in science class. ~

Pam Barclay

~ Adopted from Korea as a baby, Pam is a spunky middle-schooler who more than holds her own with her lively older brothers.

Chapter 1

Joe Savage

A headline in the *Rockdale Evening News* caught Jim Barclay's eye.

BECOME A CERTIFIED DIVER

Scuba Classes to Start Next Week

The article said that a man named Joe Savage would be teaching the 12-week course. Details of Savage's impressive background were listed.

He was a former Navy Seal. With more than 25 years of diving experience, he'd taught some 1,000 people how to dive. His program at the YMCA would combine classroom instruction and diving practice in the pool.

After graduating, the class would make a trip to the seacoast for a saltwater dive in the ocean. All students had to be at least 16 years of age. The cost was $300.

Jim had always wanted to learn to dive.

His father had once been a navy diver, and he still went diving occasionally with his friends. *If I got certified,* Jim thought, *it would be one more activity Dad and I could do together.*

There were a couple of problems, though. For one thing, Jim didn't have $300. And for another, what would his mom say? Well, there was only one way to find out.

As Jim was drying the dishes that night, he told his mother about the article.

"It's something I've always wanted to do, Mom," he said. "And since Dad dives, it's something that we could do together."

Ann smiled at her son.

"Is that why you're helping with the dishes?" she teased.

Jim blushed.

"Is it that obvious?" he asked.

"Oh, I learned how to read you a long time ago," Ann said with a grin. "Actually, Jim, I think it would be a great surprise for your father. Before we separated he wanted *me* to take a course—but I had no interest in it. What if I pay for the classes as your birthday present? We won't tell your father until you get certified. What do you say to that?"

"Oh, Mom, that's *great!* I'll go down to the Y tomorrow and sign up."

Jim's younger brother Aaron walked into the kitchen just then.

"What's Jim trying to con you out of now, Mom?" he asked suspiciously. "It must be something pretty important for him to help with the dishes."

"I'm going to take scuba lessons, little brother—but you can't tell Dad. It's going to be a surprise."

"Okay. I saw that article in the paper, too. It said that you have to be 16—otherwise, I'd take the class, too."

Ann sensed Aaron's disappointment. She gave him a hug and said, "Don't worry, honey. You'll get your chance when you're older."

The next day after school, Jim stopped

at the Y and enrolled in the scuba classes. The program was set to start the following Saturday.

* * * *

Jim arrived early for the first class. The 15 other students ranged in age from 16 to 40. Five women were in the group.

Everyone was talking when Joe Savage walked in. Lean and muscular, he wore a white T-shirt, khaki shorts, and sneakers. He looked to be in his early 40s, Jim thought, but he might be older. He was in such good physical condition that it was hard to tell.

The room quieted down as Joe introduced himself.

"Besides learning to dive, you'll learn the *principles* of diving in this course," he explained. "You'll learn about pressure and its effect on the body. You'll learn about decompression, the 'bends,' and diving medicine. And one of our classes will be devoted to the upkeep and repair of diving equipment.

"First, we'll pair everyone up with a partner. Your partner or 'buddy' will be your constant companion during this course. When you're in the water, you should always swim together. Know where your partner is at all times. That way, you'll always have help if you get into trouble. Any questions?"

Joe Savage gave the group five minutes to pair up. A man in his mid-30s had been sitting next to Jim.

He leaned over and said, "Hi. I'm Bob Snyder. Shall we be partners?"

"Sure, Bob," Jim answered. "My name is Jim Barclay."

Joe stood before the group.

"Okay, class, let's get started," he said, pointing to a chart on the wall.

"Right now we're all breathing air at atmospheric pressure. That's about 15 pounds per square inch. Every 33 feet of water increases that pressure by another 15 pounds. At a depth of 100 feet, there's almost 60 pounds of pressure on every square inch of your body."

Joe spent the next two hours lecturing. As the first class ended, Jim's hand was cramped from taking notes. He wondered when they would get into the pool.

CHAPTER 2

Shark Bait

Seven weeks later, the classes were more than half over. Joe Savage had been true to his word. The students had thoroughly studied the effect of pressure on the body. All class members had their own sets of decompression tables. This allowed them to figure safe diving times at various depths.

Joe taught them how to share one scuba tank. And he taught them how to clear their masks underwater if they ever filled with water.

In one class, the diving tanks were turned off and left at the bottom of the pool. Each student had to dive down to his or her tank, turn on the air, and strap on the tank before surfacing.

Joe stressed the importance of rising from great depths very slowly. Since the pool was only 10 feet deep, it was difficult to simulate the real thing. But Joe promised that they'd get more practice during the ocean dive.

After class one Saturday, a number of students were sitting around talking with their instructor.

"Joe, did you ever run into sharks when you were diving?" Bob Snyder asked.

Joe laughed.

"Oh, yes, a number of times," he answered. "But only once was I really scared."

"Tell us about it," Jim said.

"Well, it happened in waters off the coast of Kauai—one of the Hawaiian Islands. An air force fighter plane was coming into Kauai for a landing. But something went wrong, and it went down in the ocean just 400 yards from land. Even that close to shore, the water was 16 to 17 fathoms deep."

One of the women interrupted him.

"How deep is that, Joe?" she asked.

"A fathom is six feet—so it was about

100 feet deep there," Joe answered. "Anyway, we'd been ordered to recover the plane. My ship was at Pearl Harbor, so it took us about 10 hours to get to the crash site. We were towing a barge.

"We anchored as close as we could to the location of the crash," Joe went on. "But we couldn't find an oil slick on the water. That's how we could usually tell where a plane went down.

"Finding the plane was our first job," Joe continued. "I put four of my divers into the water along with me. I told them to swim 400 yards from the ship in four different directions. I went off the stern.

"The ocean was crystal clear that day. I'll bet we could see 75 feet underwater! I dove down 30 or 40 feet, where I could see the bottom well. Then I started to swim."

The group listened intently as Joe's voice grew softer. "Five minutes later I saw the plane on the ocean floor. The strange thing was that it didn't look damaged. In fact, if it hadn't been sitting under 100 feet of water, it could have been on an airport runway.

"All the divers carried a small yellow buoy with 150 feet of nylon line. This was to mark the plane's location. That way, we could move the ship over the crash site and begin the recovery operation.

"Anyway—I dove down and sat on the wing. I had just started to release my marking buoy. Then, in a split second, everything got dark."

Now the diving students were hanging on every word.

"It was like a large cloud had blocked the sun on a bright summer day," Joe recalled. "When I looked up, I saw three large sharks swimming about 10 to 15 feet above me!

"I thought fast. After quickly tying off my buoy, I ducked under the wing, where I felt a little safer."

Joe smiled and said, "But those darn sharks had followed me! They started to swim in circles around the plane.

"I sat there in the sand for a while, trying to decide what to do. The plane gave me some protection—but I knew I couldn't stay there much longer. Even with the double tanks we were using, my air supply wasn't going to last forever. And I still had about a 10-minute swim to get back to the ship.

"Finally, I gathered my courage and left the plane. But I decided to stay close to the ocean floor. Then at least the sharks couldn't attack me from below.

"Those sharks left the plane when I did and circled me as I swam. I was sure that one of them would dart in and bite me at any moment! And if I started to bleed—well, it could start a feeding frenzy. They'd tear me apart in no time. But for some reason that didn't happen!"

"A few minutes later I looked up and saw the hull of my ship floating 100 feet above me.

"Remember how I drilled you about the importance of coming to the surface slowly? Well, that day I broke all the rules. I put both feet on the ocean bottom and pushed off. No one ever swam to the surface any faster.

"Back on the ship, I went directly into the decompression chamber. Otherwise, I would have had the bends for sure."

Joe stopped and looked around at his students' faces.

"That's the day I thought I was going to be shark bait," he said.

"It's a good thing you didn't tell us that story at the beginning of this course, Joe," Bob Snyder said. "You might have lost half your class!"

CHAPTER 3

Graduation

Students taking the diving course were required to spend several sessions in the classroom. Joe knew they'd much rather be practicing in the pool. But it was important for them to understand certain facts about diving.

Today's lecture was on decompression sickness—also called "the bends." Joe described the compressed air a diver breathes. He said it contains higher amounts of nitrogen than people are used to. The deeper the dive—and the longer a diver stays underwater—the more nitrogen gets absorbed into the bloodstream.

As a diver rises to the surface, the water's pressure on the body lessens. That creates nitrogen bubbles in the diver's bloodstream. This expanding gas is what causes the bends. Pain and paralysis are some of the obvious symptoms. In extreme cases, death can occur.

Decompression sickness can easily be prevented by not staying in very deep water too long. Joe warned his students about rising to the surface too quickly. Instead, he advised them to come to the surface by following an air bubble. Why? An air bubble rises to the surface at about the same speed a diver should.

What if a diver accidentally stays in deep water too long? Decompressing on the way to the surface can still prevent the bends, Joe explained. Stopping at various depths on the way up allows nitrogen gases to gradually escape the bloodstream.

Finally, the classroom instruction was completed.

Joe lined up the group and said, "Are you ready to show what you know? Those of you who pass the final test today will become certified divers."

Joe himself was already wearing a full set of diving equipment.

"I want you to put your gear on now.

Then swim around on the bottom of the pool," he said. "For the next hour I'm going to pester you, one by one. Maybe I'll pull your facemask off or shut off your air supply! I may even cut your straps and take your tank away!

"If that happens, you'll need to share a tank with your partner. The point is this: I need to see how you're able to handle yourselves in emergency situations. And just remember—no matter what I do, *don't panic*! Any questions?"

The 16 students put on their gear and entered the pool. For the next 60 minutes Joe pulled every trick he knew to disrupt the divers.

But he had taught them well. No one panicked. All of them did just what they were supposed to do. In the end, Joe awarded a graduation certificate to every student. Now at last they were certified scuba divers!

After class he told the group when and where to meet for their first ocean dive.

"You'll need a wet suit," he said. "The water is just too cold to dive without one. And remember—these northern waters are not the tropics. If it's a sunny day you may be able to see 10 to 12 feet down. That's a lot less than the 60 to 70 feet you can see in the Caribbean."

* * * *

Jim was a certified scuba diver! He couldn't wait to share the news. That afternoon he called his dad and told him how he had been spending the past 12 Saturday mornings. Paul was delighted.

"Jimbo," he said, "I'm proud of you! How about this: I have to go to Fort Lauderdale on business next month. While I'm in Florida, I'm meeting up with a couple of old friends. We're going to explore a reef about 15 miles off the coast. Now that you're certified, why don't you come along?"

"I'd *love* to!" Jim shouted.

"Maybe I can get your mom, Aaron, and Pam to fly to Orlando. After we dive, we could meet them there. Then we could spend a few days at Disney World."

"Gee, this trip is sounding better all the time," Jim said.

"Well, let me work on it, son. And congratulations on your certification."

Later that afternoon Jim's mother and sister came back from shopping.

"Mom, I called Dad today and told him that I was a certified diver," Jim said excitedly. "And guess what? He's going diving in Florida next month—and he asked me to come with him."

"That's great, Jim," Ann said. "You'll have a wonderful time."

"But that's not all. Dad thought maybe the rest of the family could fly to Orlando. He and I would meet you there after we go diving. Then we could all have a few days at Disney World."

"Oh, boy, Disney World!" Pam shouted. "We can do that—can't we, Mom?"

"That does sound like fun, kids. I'll try

to work it out with your father the next time I talk to him," Ann said.

Paul called Ann the following night. They worked out arrangements for the trip to Disney World. Paul and Jim would meet them at the hotel the afternoon they arrived.

Chapter 4

Trapped

The next Saturday morning the excited group of new divers met on the dock. There they boarded an excursion boat Joe had chartered for the day.

The diving site was just a short ride from the harbor. It was about one mile offshore and protected from the wind by a small island. The water there was about 40 feet deep.

Joe knew these waters well—but there was something he didn't know. That year's winter storms had been fierce. The high winds had forced fishing trawlers to cut their nets and head for the safety of the harbor. Months had passed since the storms—but those abandoned nets were still drifting around in the ocean currents.

Joe spoke to his students when they reached the dive site.

"At this depth, you should be able to

stay down for about an hour," he said. "Remember to stay with your partner. And don't go more than 300 yards from the boat. Now jump in and have fun!"

Eight pairs of divers immediately went over the side of the boat.

Jim was surprised at how cloudy the water seemed. And Joe had been right—he could see only about 10 feet in front of him.

Staying near the bottom, Bob Snyder started swimming east. Jim struggled to keep up with him, wondering what his hurry was. He was afraid to let Bob get too far ahead of him. It would be easy to lose him in the darkness.

As Jim got closer, he sensed that Bob was having a problem. Oh, no! Bob had swum into an abandoned fishing net!

The more Jim's partner struggled, the more tangled up he became. The heavy net was holding him down under 40 feet of murky water!

Jim had to think fast. He needed a

knife to cut Bob free, but he'd have to leave him to go get one.

Jim was worried. *What if he runs out of air before I get back?* he thought to himself. *What if I can't even find him again in this murky water?*

It didn't take long for Jim to make a decision. He'd take off his tank and leave it with Bob as a spare. It was only 40 feet to the surface. He knew he could get there without a tank.

Once he reached the surface, he'd take a bearing on the shoreline before swimming back to the boat. There he could get another set of scuba tanks and a knife before swimming back and trying to free his partner. Hopefully, Joe Savage would be there to help him.

Jim popped to the surface and hungrily sucked in a big breath of air. He looked at the shoreline and located a small cottage on the beach. That would be his reference point for finding his way back. Then he started swimming toward the boat.

When Jim climbed on board, the boat operator was the only one there. Joe Savage had dived in to check on a couple of other divers. Jim told the boat operator what had happened. Then he quickly put on another set of diving gear and found a sharp knife.

Within minutes he was back in the water. As Jim swam, he kept an eye on the beach cottage. When his position looked about right, he dove.

When he reached the bottom, there was no sign of Bob or the abandoned net. *He's got to be nearby,* Jim thought to himself. *I just have to keep looking.*

Jim searched for several minutes, but saw nothing. Then, just as he was becoming discouraged, he spotted the abandoned net.

Being careful not to get entangled, he swam alongside it for 40 yards. Then he spotted Bob just ahead.

His partner looked like a fly trapped in a spider web! He was also breathing from the extra tank Jim had left with him. His original tank must have already gone dry!

Bob forced a smile when he realized that his partner had come back. Jim cut the net quickly and carefully. In a couple of minutes he had Bob freed, and they headed for the surface.

But the long struggle with the heavy net had exhausted Bob. He was in no condition to make the long swim back to the boat—but he wouldn't have to.

Joe Savage was waving from the boat deck! He had returned to the boat along with all the other divers. As soon as they spotted Jim and Bob on the surface, they brought the boat to them.

After they were safely aboard, Joe approached Jim.

"Congratulations, son!" Joe said. "You handled yourself very well today. You had to make a lot of quick decisions—and, in my opinion, you made the correct ones. Your partner owes you his life."

"Thanks a lot, Joe," Jim said. "Coming

from you, that means a lot."

On the bus ride back to Rockdale, Bob Snyder said, "Jim, I don't know how to thank you for what you did for me today. If you ever need anything, you call me."

He reached into his wallet and gave Jim his business card.

Then Bob added, "I know! Didn't I hear you say that you didn't have a wet suit? Joe let you borrow one, didn't he?"

"Yeah," Jim answered.

"Well, my friend, I'm going to write you a check for $250. Tomorrow you can go out and buy one."

"Oh, no, Bob—I can't take your money," Jim protested.

"Of course you can," Bob laughed. "It's the very least I can do."

CHAPTER 5

Sea Snakes

The bus was about to pull into Rockdale when one of the class members stood up. Joan Peterson got everyone's attention before she spoke.

"I'm sure you all agree that this course has been a great experience," Joan said. "I've enjoyed meeting all of you. So before we go our separate ways, I'd like to invite you for a cookout. It will be at my house on Monday evening. Joe won't be leaving town until Tuesday, so he'll be there, too!"

The divers cheered. Everyone thought it was a great idea! Soon, members of the group were offering to bring things to the potluck—hamburgers, potato salad, cold drinks, desserts.

Joan gave everyone her address and said, "Great! I'll see you all around 6 o'clock on Monday."

The cookout was a huge success.

Everyone was in great spirits.

When dinner was over, Bob Snyder turned to Joe Savage. "Joe," he asked, "did you ever have any more frightening experiences when you were diving?"

Joe thought for a moment and said, "Oh, I suppose I have—but only one comes to mind."

"Tell us about it!" Bob said eagerly.

Everyone sat back and listened as Joe started to tell his story.

"I was a navy salvage diver back then. Our ship was in the East China Sea, heading south on its way to Hong Kong. As we were going through the Formosa Straits, we received an urgent message. A Taiwanese freighter had gone aground. According to the radio report, it was stranded on a sandbar on the southern tip of Taiwan. The message said: EMERGENCY ASSISTANCE REQUIRED. PROCEED AT ONCE.

"Navy diving vessels did a lot of salvage work in those days. Although they weren't very fast ships, they all had big propellers and could generate great power.

"Our aim was to get our two-inch towing cable over to the freighter. Then we'd wait for high tide and try to pull it off the sandbar."

Everyone was listening closely as Joe continued.

"But we ran into a serious problem," he continued. "The stranded vessel was grounded in 12 feet of water. Our ship needed 17 feet of water in order to navigate. So we couldn't get within 400 yards of the freighter. We were baffled. How were we going to get our towing cable over to the other ship?

"Then I had an idea. It occurred to me that a powerful swimmer could reach the freighter while towing 400 feet of lightweight, nylon cord. Once on board, the cord could be used to pull over a heavier, quarter-inch rope.

"Then, we could use the quarter-inch rope to pull over an even heavier rope, strong enough to pull the towing cable.

Our captain agreed that it worth a try. Since I was the strongest swimmer, I volunteered to do the job.

"The swim was difficult and tiring. A fairly heavy sea was running. As the nylon strung out behind me, it was casting quite a drag. It took me more than half an hour to reach the freighter! That's when I realized I faced yet another problem.

"The shallower water was raising the waves more than 12 feet. One moment I'd be almost staring into the eyes of the Chinese sailors. But the next moment I'd be looking 15 feet *up* to them!

"The crew had put a rope ladder over the side for me. My only chance was to grab onto the ladder at the very top of a wave and then to hang on for dear life as the water went out from under me.

"It was a dangerous maneuver! If I misjudged a wave, I'd be pounded against the steel hull of the ship.

"To get the timing right, I rode up and down on several surges. Then, at the crest of the next wave, I swam close to the hull and grabbed the ladder. When the wave went out from under me, I hung in the air as I tried to get my feet onto the ladder. It worked! Moments later, I climbed on the deck, the nylon cord still tied to my waist.

"Once I got on board, all I heard was a clamor of Chinese. 'Does anyone speak English?' I shouted. A young sailor stepped out of the group. 'I do,' he said. Then I asked him what everyone was shouting about. 'They say you are a very brave man—and maybe a little crazy, too,' the Chinese sailor told me.

"'It was a long swim,' I said. 'But I don't think it was *that* big a deal!

"'Oh, no,' he said. 'It's not the swim they're applauding—it's your escape from *them*.' As he pointed at a wave, I looked down at 10 or 12 large Asian sea snakes! 'Very poisonous. They kill many people,' the Chinese sailor explained.

"I was so shocked I fell against a bulkhead. I hadn't even *seen* the snakes while I was in the water! My mind was on getting the ship off the sandbar. Now I knew for sure I wasn't *swimming* back. I'd join the Chinese navy first!

"Our plan worked. Some hours later we finally had the tow wire secured. On the next high tide, we pulled the freighter into deep water. Then, we followed her back to port—just in case she had some hull damage. But luckily, the freighter was fine. She made the trip without a problem."

"Wow! That's quite a story, Joe," Bob Snyder said.

The other divers quickly agreed.

Chapter 6

Preparing to Dive

The day finally came for Jim to fly to Fort Lauderdale to meet his dad. He spotted his father waiting at the gate.

"Hi, Dad!" Jim called out.

"Jimbo," was all his father said as he grabbed his son in a big bear hug.

As they were driving to the motel, Jim turned to his father. "How deep will we be diving tomorrow, Dad?"

"I think the reef runs 70 to 80 feet," Paul answered.

"Gee, I hope I do okay. I've never been down more than 40 feet, you know."

"Don't worry, son, you'll be fine. And wait till you see how clear the water is down here! We should see all kinds of underwater life."

"At that depth, won't we run out of air pretty quick?" Jim asked.

"We'll be using big double tanks, Jim,"

Paul answered. "That's enough air for an hour and 15 or 20 minutes."

"I can hardly wait!" Jim replied.

That evening over dinner, Jim told his dad about Bob Snyder getting trapped in the fishing net.

"Everyone said that I saved his life," he added modestly.

"Well, it sounds as if you did, son. You certainly made all the right decisions. No one should ever dive without a knife. You'll have one with you tomorrow, that's for sure."

The next morning after breakfast, Paul and Jim drove down to the harbor. Fred McCabe and Walt Coles were two of Paul's oldest and dearest friends. The three men had attended college together and remained friends through the years. Jim had met them about six years ago when they visited Rockdale. Today, Fred and Walt had the same comment when they saw Paul's oldest son.

"What happened to that skinny little

kid we met six years ago?" they laughingly asked Paul.

Grinning, Paul said, "The boy grew up some, didn't he?"

Fred lived in Fort Lauderdale. He owned the *Sea Witch,* a 28-foot cabin cruiser. When Jim saw it, he was very impressed. It was a great diving boat with a large, open deck. There was lots of room for all their diving gear and plenty of power to get back to the harbor quickly if bad weather kicked up.

Fred had rigged the *Sea Witch* for diving. Racks on the stern held 10 sets of double tanks. There were also six single tanks and more flippers, face masks, and weight belts than Jim had ever seen.

"Wow, Mr. McCabe, you have enough gear here to start a business!" Jim said.

"First of all, Jimmy, call me Fred. And to tell the truth, I thought about that. But that would make diving *work*. I want it to be fun! So I decided not to take strangers diving or even to teach diving. Instead, I'm only going diving with my friends—like your old man."

Walt Coles winked at Jim. "But in your father's case," he added, "we usually have to teach him a few things. He's a slow learner, you know."

Jim had to laugh. His good friends in high school teased each other just like this. It was nice to see that guys still kidded around even as they got older.

Fred McCabe started the engine, and the *Sea Witch* roared to life. She moved slowly from the pier and headed for the open ocean. Once past the harbor entrance, Fred added power and the bow cut through the sea at 20 knots.

Walt and Paul, with Jim looking over their shoulders, were busy studying a navigational chart.

"This reef runs about 10 miles parallel to the coastline," Walt said. "Although the depth is only 70 feet or so, not many divers come out here."

"Why's that?" Paul asked.

"It's 15 miles offshore and not visible from land. Most people don't want to come out this far," Walt answered. "You never know what you'll see out here."

"Maybe a sunken pirate ship," Jim said teasingly.

"Don't laugh, son," Walt replied. "A good many old ships have sunk in these waters—and most of them have never been found."

The *Sea Witch* covered the 15 miles in just under an hour. By 10 o'clock in the morning they were anchored in 75 feet of water. It was a spectacular day—bright sunshine, almost no wind, and hardly a ripple on the water.

Fred secured the boat. Then he smiled and said, "Jimmy, you picked a great day to dive. Even though you can only see at most 100 feet underwater, it's going to *feel* like miles!"

CHAPTER 7

The Reef

Jim had never worn double tanks before. They felt a lot heavier.

His father reassured him. "Once you get in the water, you won't notice the difference," he said.

By 10:30, all four divers were rigged up and ready to go. No wet suits were necessary in these waters, but each man wore a belt holding a 7-inch knife.

A whole new world opened up to Jim when he hit the tropical waters. Fred was right—it felt like he could see for miles! Compared to his dive up north, it was unbelievable. The reef was alive with fish —*thousands* of fish in all shapes, colors, and sizes. And there were amazing coral formations that Jim had only seen in pictures.

Paul was swimming alongside his son. He sensed Jim's awe at the new world he was seeing for the first time. Motioning for

Jim to follow him, he headed north along the reef. Jim was so busy watching the sea floor, he didn't see the huge school of amberjacks swimming toward him. Then suddenly, he was in the midst of thousands of fish! Some came so close he could almost touch them.

On the reef below, Jim saw a group of barracuda. They were searching the coral formations for an easy meal. Moments later, he spied a giant grouper that had to weigh 50 pounds or more. Jim was thrilled. *This is what diving is all about,* he thought to himself.

For the next 30 minutes Jim and his dad floated through the spectacular underwater paradise. Occasionally, one of the others would swim down to the reef to pick up a memento of the dive. But mostly, they hovered 20 or 30 feet above the reef enjoying the beauty that few people ever get a chance to see.

Then Jim spotted a large school of parrot fish on the ocean floor. They seemed to be feeding on some kind of marine growth attached to the coral. The brightly colored fish were green, red, and yellow. He couldn't remember when he'd seen anything more beautiful. These bottom feeders paid no attention to the divers staring down at them.

Paul tapped his son on the shoulder. Then he pointed out a moray eel just 20 feet below them. Waiting for an unlucky fish to swim by, its head was sticking out of an opening in the coral reef. Jim had read that moray eels had jaws like a pit bull. They could be very dangerous if provoked.

Paul checked his watch and his air gauge. He wanted to be sure that they had plenty of air left when they headed back toward the boat. The gauge showed that only one quarter of the air had been used. Good! That meant they could swim for another 10 or 15 minutes before starting back for the boat.

As they continued north, Jim saw a big

manta ray. Slowly flapping its huge wings, it glided through the sea in slow motion. Jim was following this great fish when he realized he'd come to the edge of the reef. No longer was he looking down 30 feet to the reef bottom. Now he was staring into 400 feet of utter darkness!

As he turned to head back, something caught his eye. A huge object of some kind was off the edge of the reef, resting on a ledge another 40 feet down. It looked like the remains of a sunken ship! He motioned to his father. Together, they swam down to have a closer look. The wrecked ship was covered with sea growth. It looked like it had been there for some time. It wasn't a sleek ship, but rather a wooden hulled vessel, maybe 50 feet long. If it hadn't hung up on the ledge, it would have plummeted 400 feet to the ocean floor.

On the ship's starboard side, they discovered a large hole in the hull. Jim couldn't resist swimming over and peeking in. Then he noticed that Paul was signaling him to swim back up to the reef. But as he turned to follow his father, Jim felt something wrap around his ankle! He looked down and gasped in horror. A big, black tentacle had wrapped around his leg. And it was trying to pull him into the sunken hull!

CHAPTER 8

Tentacles of Terror

Jim was slowly being dragged into the dark hole! He didn't know what kind of creature it was—but it was very strong. He struggled to get away, but couldn't.

Paul had seen the powerful tentacle grab his son. He drew out his knife and swam down to him. Jim was bracing his feet on the wooden planks around the hole, fighting to stay on the outside of the hull.

Paul cut the tentacle clutching Jim's ankle. But just as he did, a second tentacle shot out of the darkness and wrapped around his waist. Then a third grabbed his right leg. Paul realized then that they'd stumbled into the lair of a giant squid!

Jim was now trying to help his father. Both of them hacked away at the black arms. But it seemed that as soon as they got free of one tentacle, another one would grab them. Rows of suction cups on the underside of each tentacle helped the creature grip its prey.

By now, both Jim and Paul were halfway inside the sunken hull. In the struggle, one of the flailing tentacles had ripped off Jim's face mask. Oh, no! Now, on top of everything else, he had lost his ability to see clearly!

Paul didn't notice. He was too busy fighting the creature in front of him to think about two more possible dangers. The water around them had become red with blood and bits of flesh. Any sharks in the area would be attracted by the smell. Stimulated by the blood, they would be even more dangerous than the beast they were now battling.

And their air supply was running low! Instead of swimming easily at a depth of 40 or 50 feet, they'd been struggling at a depth of 120 feet. The increased depth and physical activity had used up their air at a much faster pace.

Finally, Paul found himself totally free. He grabbed Jim's arm and quickly pulled him toward the opening in the hull. Once outside the wreck, Paul saw that one long, black tentacle was still wrapped around Jim's leg. He reached out and made one final cut to free his son.

Again Paul looked at his air gauge—it registered empty! Halfway to the surface, they took their last breath from the tanks. Then, with their lungs crying for oxygen, they broke the surface and desperately gasped for air.

Back aboard the *Sea Witch,* Fred and Walt had been scanning the water with binoculars. They'd returned to the boat 10 minutes ago with almost empty air tanks.

Fred was worried. "They must be out of air by now," he said. "Where are they?"

At just that moment, Walt spotted two heads popping to the surface. He pointed and shouted. The Barclays were only about 400 yards north of the boat.

"There they are!" he cried out. "Pull

anchor and let's get over there!"

As father and son bobbed in the waves, Jim looked at Paul and said, "What *was* that?"

"That was a giant squid, son. Not a very friendly guy, was he?"

"You can say that again," was all Jim could think of to say.

CHAPTER 9

Back on the *Sea Witch*

Fred slowed the *Sea Witch* and brought it alongside the two divers. Walt helped them climb the ladder into the boat. They were both exhausted from their long battle.

Fred looked at them and said, "Did you have a run-in with a squid?"

Paul looked surprised. "How did you know that?"

"Mostly from those round, red welts on your bodies," Fred answered. "They look like they were made by the suction cups on a squid's tentacles."

"Well, you're exactly right, Fred. We met a *big* one—and he wanted us for dinner!"

For the next hour, Paul and Jim sat on the deck, telling the story of their battle.

After hearing all the details, Walt said, "You have all the luck, Paul. All I saw were a few fish."

Paul looked at his friend and burst out laughing. "I'd trade you a peaceful dive watching fish for what we've just been through anytime!"

Fred now looked over at Jim. "Tell me, Jimmy. How do you like diving now?"

"I'm really not sure," Jim answered. "I do know that I've never been more frightened in my life."

"Son," his father said, "don't feel bad. I've never been more frightened either."

Shifting the gearshift into drive, Fred headed the *Sea Witch* back toward the harbor. It had been quite a day. On the way in, Jim marveled at the unbelievable beauty of the ocean. The sights he'd seen on the reef floor today had been truly spectacular. But at the same time the sea held hidden dangers. *It was a world that humans were not born to enter,* Jim thought to himself. *Only with the assistance of modern diving equipment could we explore this strange frontier.*

Jim promised himself to always remember and respect the dangers that lurked below the surface. He'd never be reckless. And he'd faithfully follow every safety rule Joe Savage had taught him.

It was late afternoon when Fred guided his boat into its slip. After cleaning up the deck and rinsing it with fresh water, they put away the diving gear—all except the air tanks. When they left the boat, Fred would drop them off to be recharged with air.

Paul invited everyone to join him for dinner that evening. Over big steaks, the story of their battle with the squid was retold dramatically.

Walt smiled and looked fondly at his friend's son. "You know, Jim, every time you tell that story, the squid gets bigger. I'll bet by next year that creature will be as big as Godzilla!"

Everyone laughed. Even Jim smiled, knowing they were teasing him.

After finishing dinner, Paul and Jim said goodbye.

"Next time you're in town, let's do this again," Fred said.

"Great!" Paul answered. "Just remind me to stay away from sunken ships."

Chapter 10

Orlando

Paul and Jim slept late the next morning. They had nothing to do until meeting the rest of the family that afternoon. The trip to Orlando was about a four-hour drive up the Florida Turnpike.

Ann and the kids were due to arrive in Orlando at 3 o'clock. Paul figured that it would take them another hour to get their bags and check into the hotel. If he and Jim left Fort Lauderdale by noon, they should get to the hotel about the same time the rest of the family did.

After breakfast, Paul said, "What do you want to do, son? We have about three hours to kill."

"Isn't the Swimming Hall of Fame in Fort Lauderdale?" Jim asked.

"Yes, I think it is," his father answered.

"Could we stop there for a visit?" Jim asked. "I've always wanted to see it."

"Sure," Paul answered. "Let's go."

Jim had always enjoyed watching the swimming events during the Olympic Games. Being an athlete himself, he knew how hard world-class swimmers had to train. They had almost no body fat and unbelievable endurance. To Jim, there was nothing more graceful than a strong swimmer slicing through the water—especially a butterflier. In his opinion, the butterfly was the most challenging of all the strokes. Jim had always thought that butterfliers looked like sleek dolphins slipping through the water.

Jim had often wished Rockdale High School had a swim team. But with his dedication to football, he wouldn't have had time for swimming anyway.

The visit to the Hall of Fame was a great treat. All the famous names in swimming were there. Standing at the sprinter's wall, Jim couldn't believe how race times had improved in 50 years. In the 1930s, the great Johnny Weismuller struggled to break 1 minute in the 100-yard freestyle. These days swimmers were covering the distance in under 45 seconds.

After visiting most of the displays in the Hall, Paul checked his watch. "I think we'd better get going," he said. "We still have a four-hour drive ahead of us."

"Okay, Dad," Jim answered. "Thanks a lot for bringing me here. I'm so glad I got to see this place."

In the car, their conversation again turned to yesterday's dive.

"Gosh," Jim said, "that reef was absolutely beautiful. I never expected to see so much marine life."

"Yeah, Jim, it sure was. Too bad the squid kind of ruined the trip."

"No, Dad, it didn't ruin the trip at all! If anything, it made it more exciting."

"You know, son," Paul said, "it might be a good idea if you didn't tell your mom about the squid. For some reason, our trips always seem to involve some danger. I think your mom worries about you. That story might make her think twice about your diving."

"I guess you're right, Dad. We'll leave the squid out of the story."

At about 4 o'clock, Paul and Jim pulled into the hotel parking lot. Ann and the other two kids were already there, relaxing at the pool.

"Daddy!" Pam shouted as Paul walked into the pool area.

"Hi, Buttons. Do you know that you get prettier every time I see you?" her father said as he gave her a hug.

Aaron jumped out of the pool and ran up to his father.

"Hi, Dad," he said, as Paul gave him a big hug.

"Aaron, how are you doing?" Paul said.

Then, before Aaron could answer, Paul walked over to Ann.

He bent down and kissed her on the cheek. "And *you* get prettier every time I see you, too," he said.

Ann smiled. "Is that so?" she said. "I

think you've been breathing too much of that compressed air."

"Jim, how was the diving trip?" Aaron jumped in.

"It was really great," Jim answered.

For the next hour or so, he told them about the reef dive. The only thing he left out was any mention of the squid!

Chapter 11

Universal Studios

The next morning after breakfast, the Barclays headed for Disney World. They weren't surprised by the long lines for all the major rides. They had a great day, anyway. By 4 o'clock, they were tired and ready to leave the park. They'd been on all the rides except the Submarine.

On the way back to the hotel, Aaron said, "I wonder if there was a giant squid on the submarine ride." Jim turned around and smiled at his dad.

Ann saw the smile and wondered what it meant.

That evening over dinner, Aaron said, "Let's go to Universal Studios tomorrow."

"That might be fun," Ann said. "The rides there are supposed to be very realistic."

Paul was in great spirits. He always enjoyed having his whole family together.

"Universal Studios it is," he said.

The next morning they took a bus from the hotel to Universal Studios. The place had been designed to look exactly like a Hollywood film lot. In fact, all the rides were keyed to one movie or another.

First, they rode in the car used in the *Back to the Future* movie. They took a monorail ride that King Kong attacked. And they went on another ride from the movie, *ET*. In between rides they walked around sightseeing, eating hot dogs and popcorn.

The most popular ride had the longest line, of course. On this ride, the boat is attacked by the shark from the movie, *Jaws*. Aaron and Pam pleaded with their parents to go on that one.

Paul finally said, "Okay, okay. We'll just bite the bullet and stand in line as long as it takes."

An hour later, they climbed into the boat that was going to be attacked by a 25-foot shark. They motored slowly from the dock and started across the lagoon. Suddenly—out of nowhere—a huge mechanical shark reared out of the water. Its huge mouth was wide open, and it looked as if it could devour the entire boat. All the passengers screamed! Then the shark dove, but not before thoroughly splashing everyone with water.

Around the next bend in the waterway, the shark reappeared. It was still just as frightening, and Aaron was terrified.

His eyes were wide as he turned to his parents. "Have you ever *seen* anything as scary as that?"

Jim looked at his father and grinned.

He couldn't help himself. "Well, as a matter of fact we have," he said.

Again, the ever-sharp Ann noticed her son's sly grin. She *knew* that it meant something. *Sooner or later, I'll find out what this is all about,* she thought to herself.

That evening after dinner, the Barclay kids were busy watching a TV show.

Ann saw her chance. She quietly said to

Paul, "Can we have a talk?"

"Sure," Paul said nervously.

Somehow she always seemed to know what he was thinking. *How does she do that?* he wondered.

When they were sitting by the pool, Ann said, "What really happened on that dive you and Jim made?"

Paul gulped. "Jim told you the whole story yesterday," he said innocently.

"Jim told a story—but I don't think it was the *whole* story," Ann answered.

Paul couldn't lie to Ann. He told her all about the squid. When he was finished, tears were running down her cheeks.

"What's the matter?" Paul asked.

"Don't you understand?" she said. "You and Jim are two of the most important people in my life. I don't want to lose either of you! Something like this seems to happen every time you and the kids go off on a trip! You always seem to get into enough trouble for a hundred people!"

"Yeah," Paul sighed. "I guess we run into more than our share of difficult situations, all right. What if I stop taking the kids on trips for a while?"

Ann dried her tears. "That might not be a bad idea," she said.

Just then Jim, Aaron, and Pam came running out to the pool. Aaron was the first to speak.

"Guess what, Dad?" Aaron cried. "We saw an ad on TV about a trip down the Amazon River in dugout canoes. Doesn't that sound like a great idea for our next adventure?"

Ann looked over at Paul and slowly shook her head.

Then she threw up her arms and said, "This family will be the death of me yet!"

COMPREHENSION QUESTIONS

Who and Where?

1. Where did Jim go to take scuba diving lessons?
2. What former Navy Seal was the diving instructor?
3. Who got entangled in an abandoned fishing net?
4. To help him find his way, who used a beach cottage as a reference point?
5. From what body of water did Joe help rescue a stranded freighter?
6. Where had the giant squid been hiding?
7. Near what city is Disney World located?
8. In what city is the Swimming Hall of Fame located?

Remembering Details

1. Why couldn't Aaron take diving lessons with Jim?

2. What do divers use to mark the location of a crash site?
3. What's the common name for decompression sickness?
4. What did Bob Snyder insist on buying for Jim?
5. What was the name of Fred McCabe's cabin cruiser?
6. What creature glides through the sea by flapping its giant wings?
7. How could Fred tell that the Barclays had fought off a giant squid?